MADAME DE

LOUISE DE VILMORIN

Madame de

TRANSLATED BY
DUFF COOPER

With drawings by
IAN RIBBONS

COLLINS
ST JAMES'S PLACE LONDON
1952

PRINTED IN GREAT BRITAIN
COLLINS CLEAR-TYPE PRESS: LONDON AND GLASGOW

To
Andrée de Vilmorin

Madame de

W HENEVER love touches history, events of the
past belong to the present.

Elegance rather than beauty was accounted the
mark of merit in the circle of society to which
Madame de   belonged and in that circle
Madame de   herself was acknowledged to be
of all women the most elegant. She set the fashion
among those who knew her and, as the men said

she was inimitable, sensible
women sought to imitate her.
They hoped that some glint
of her lustre might shine on
them, and that their ears might
catch some echo of the adulation
she received. Wherever her
approval fell, distinction was
conferred ; she was original in
all her ways ; she made the
commonplace seem rare, and
she always did what nobody
expected.

Monsieur de   was a

rich man. He was proud of his wife and refused her
nothing. He never questioned her about the money
she spent, so she had no cause to fear his reproaches,
yet from a sort of weakness, not unmixed with a
desire to prove her cleverness, when he admired
some object she had just bought or a dress she was
wearing for the first time, she could not resist saying
that it had cost her half of what she had actually paid
for it. So Madame de   hid from Monsieur
de   the total amount of the bills that she was
incurring. After this had been going on for a few
years she found herself seriously in debt, which
caused her at first anxiety, then anguish and finally
despair. It was the more difficult for her to find the
courage to tell her husband because she had been
deceiving him for so long, and because he had
always treated her with the greatest generosity.
Unwilling to lose either his admiration or his
confidence, she decided that the secret sale of some
jewellery was the only way in which she could solve
her problem.

It would be unwise, she thought, to get rid of
an heirloom, or of a large number of jewels of inferior
value, owing to the difficulty of accounting for their
disappearance ; so she decided, when she had gone
through her jewel case, to sell a pair of earrings made
of two superb diamonds, cut in the shape of hearts.
It had been a splendid present which Monsieur de
          had given her on the day after their marriage.

She called on her jeweller. He was a thoroughly
reliable man ; in the houses of many of his most
important customers he was as much a friend as a

jeweller. She swore him to secrecy, and spoke to him in such a way that he received the impression that Monsieur de   was aware of what his wife was doing. The jeweller assumed that Monsieur de   had some private money troubles, and wishing to help him without letting Madame de realise what he suspected, he tactfully asked :

"But, Madame, what will you say to Monsieur de   ?"

"Oh," she answered, "I shall tell him I've lost them."

"You are so charming that I am sure people always believe whatever you say," said the jeweller, and he bought the earrings.

Madame de   paid her debts, and her beauty, free of care, shone brighter than ever.

At a ball a week later Madame de   suddenly clasped her hands to her ears and cried out :

9

"Heavens, I've lost my earrings! They must have fallen off while I was dancing."

Several people who had stopped dancing and were standing round said she had not been wearing them that evening.

"Yes, I was. I'm sure I had them," she said, and still hiding her ears with her hands she ran to her husband.

"My earrings! My two hearts! I've lost them! They fell off! Look, look," she cried, removing her hands.

"You were not wearing your earrings this evening," replied Monsieur de   . "I am absolutely sure of it. I noticed it when we left, and as we were already very late I was careful not to mention it, for I was afraid you would send for them and make us still later."

"You are wrong. I know you are," she answered. "I hesitated whether to put on my hearts or my emeralds and it was my hearts that I chose."

"Then you must have left them on your dressing table. I was hurrying you and you didn't notice what you were doing," said Monsieur de
and after a moment's pause he went on, "Are you sure you weren't holding them in your hand, meaning to put them on in the carriage, as you sometimes do?"

"In the carriage? They may have fallen in the carriage," she said, "but I think it unlikely."

She seemed terribly upset. Monsieur de
begged her to wait calmly, and in his anxiety to set her mind at rest sent for lanterns and went out

himself to make a thorough search of the carriage. He then drove home, where he looked in the jewel case. When his search proved vain he rang the bell, and woke up the servants. He questioned his wife's maid.

" I can't remember for certain," she replied, " but I've never seen Madame go out in the evening without her earrings."

Since the earrings were not in the house it followed that Madame de   must have taken them with her. Monsieur de   could form no other conclusion. Worried and empty-handed he returned to the ball. There he found an atmosphere of distress, doubt and embarrassment. Nobody liked to dance, the band stopped playing and the evening came to an end.

On the following day there were paragraphs in the morning papers referring to the incident and giving the impression that it was a question of theft. The jeweller found himself in the unpleasant position of not being able to divulge the secret which had made him the honest possessor of jewels that were now believed to have been stolen. After an hour's cogitation he put the earrings in a case and called at the house of Monsieur de   , who received him immediately.

"I'm sure you've come to tempt me," said Monsieur de   , welcoming him.

"I wish I had, my dear sir," replied the jeweller, "but not to-day. I've never been so put out as this morning and before bothering you, offending you perhaps, I must appeal to your discretion."

"A secret?" asked Monsieur de   .

"A secret, and a question of conscience," said the jeweller.

Monsieur de   looked him straight in the eyes.

"I will be discreet," he answered. "I promise. Speak. I'm listening."

The jeweller then told him how he had been visited by Madame de   , how she had brought him the diamond hearts and how, not being able to believe that she was selling such valuable jewels without the knowledge of her husband, he had thought he was doing them both a service when he made the purchase. With these words he took the case out of his pocket, opened it and added:

"You will understand my feelings when I read in the papers this morning that it was suspected that these earrings had been stolen."

Although Monsieur de   was sad to learn that for a long time his wife had been misleading him and that by concealing her debts she had done harm to his credit and his good name; although he was shocked by the cold-blooded deception that she had practised the evening before at the ball, by the silence with which she had accepted the rumours that were going round the town and by her hypocrisy in pretending to be unhappy, yet he gave no sign of what he was feeling but thanked the jeweller for having called. They exchanged a few masculine jokes about the unreliability of women, even the most reliable ones, after which Monsieur de   bought back the earrings.

"I'm sorry to have to sell them to you for the second time," said the jeweller.

Monsieur de   laughed. "Don't apologise," he said, "I'm delighted to have got them back."

Monsieur de   had a mistress, a beautiful Spanish lady with whom he was beginning to fall out of love. It happened that she was leaving on that very day for South America, and as Madame de   had shown by selling her diamond hearts that she set small store by them, it seemed to him that he could not do better than give them to this beautiful lady, as though to reward her for going away before putting him to the trouble of breaking with her. She accepted them quite naturally as though there were nothing unusual in his making her such a valuable present, and this flattered Monsieur de   's vanity. He took her to the station and saw her into her compartment. As he walked down the platform she leant out of the carriage window and as the train left he replied to her gestures of farewell by putting his gloves to his lips and waving them as though to shower her with kisses. Then he went home.

He found Madame de   alone in her small sitting room, where she was having tea and reading the evening papers.

"Don't you think," he asked, "that they are making

13

much too much fuss about an incident which, regrettable though it is, can interest nobody but ourselves."

"I agree with you," she answered, "the press is very tiresome."

"Do you suspect anyone?" he asked.

"No, nobody, nobody," she replied, "and the more I think of it the more I am inclined to believe that you were right. But if only you had said to me when we were going out last night that I hadn't got my earrings on, I shouldn't have been so absentminded. I was late and I must have had them in my hand to put them on in the carriage. And then I forgot about them. You were talking, weren't you? And they must have fallen down while I was putting my gloves on, or they may have caught in my lace shawl, and perhaps they fell on the pavement when we got out and some passer-by picked them up. In any case it was my fault. It was stupid of me. It

has been a bother and a worry for you. I'm so sorry ;
you must forgive me."

" Forgive ? " said Monsieur de   .

" Forgive," she repeated.

" Say it again," he said.

She thought he must be getting deaf, and cried :
" Forgive, forgive."

Monsieur de   said he would think it over.
They looked into one another's eyes and a long
silence fell between them. They remained so, motionless, hardly breathing, until they were interrupted
by the entry of a footman bringing logs for the fire.
There was a note of irritation in Monsieur de   's
voice as he said :

" Well, if you don't suspect anybody, do put a
stop to all this chatter, all these inquiries and rumours."

" But how can I ? " she asked.

" Are you quite certain that you lost the jewellery ? "

" Yes," she said.

" Then," he replied, " you must say that you've
found it again."

Troubled by the consequences of her falsehood,
and ready to say anything to stop people talking,
Madame de   wrote forthwith at her husband's
dictation a statement for publication in the press.

To people who congratulated her on having found
her earrings she said, " I shan't wear them in future
except at home. I'm too frightened of losing them
again."

In the evenings she wore some other diamonds
that she had inherited. Few people noticed the
change and the incident was forgotten.

Shortly afterwards the lovely Spanish lady landed in South America. During the crossing she had wisely kept at a distance young men, of uncertain future, whose hearts had caught fire from the light in her dark eyes, and at the end of the journey there had been no candidate of sufficient importance to take the place in her life that had been occupied by Monsieur de   . Alone in a big city she began to fall in love with the memory of the man whom she had not loved when she might have, and sadly she scattered on the gaming table the golden coins that he had given her. At first she won large sums and then she spent night after night wrestling with Fortune. But Fortune, as she ever does, proved fickle. She came to her only every other night, then only once a week, then never. The lovely Spanish lady sought for her at every table and at every Casino. She lost every one of those golden coins without finding her, and in order to go on searching she had to sell the diamond earrings which Monsieur de   had given her.

They had hardly shone for an hour in the shop window of the principal jeweller of the city before they caught the eye of a rich European diplomat who had just been appointed Ambassador to a country that was a neighbour of his own. He bought them for their beauty and sailed the next day. He was a man who enjoyed all the advantages which wealth, rank and intelligence can confer, and his arrival at his new post created quite a stir of interest. At the first dinner party that one of his colleagues gave in his honour he found himself sitting next to Madame de   . He admired her and found her entertaining. She knew how to interest men. He was fascinated and showed it. She, too, was attracted. There was nothing that gave her greater pleasure than the admiration of others. It was a pleasure of which she never tired. And the Ambassador gave her this pleasure from the first evening they met. Her vanity was aroused. He had no eyes for any other woman.

The fact was recognised by everybody. As they belonged to the same coterie of the same society they saw each other frequently at dinners, balls and receptions, and each time they met, without ever offending convention or giving cause for scandal by the length of their conversation, they would have a few words together, moving away from the throng as though they had to talk about something of immediate importance.

Every morning the Ambassador sent Madame de   a short letter and he called on her every afternoon. Although she was very pleased by these attentions she remained for some time uncertain as to her own feelings towards him. But when one evening he excused himself from calling she was more keenly disappointed than she would admit even to herself. It came to her as a revelation. Henceforth, whenever Madame de   felt herself in danger of yielding to this persistent courtship, she would say she was ill, would shut up her house and go to the country, or pay a short visit with her husband to some sunny seaside resort. This behaviour, whether due to fantasy or virtue, served only to increase the Ambassador's passion, all the more so because during these absences she wrote him letters which without being love-letters were full of love.

These letters which brought him violets, blossoms of mimosa and grains of sand proved that she was thinking of him on her walks and that he was never far from her mind during those days of exile.

It amused Monsieur de   to tease his wife about this friendship. When he spoke of the Ambassador he referred to him as "your suitor," which made her smile. Believing her to be incapable either of doing wrong or of feeling passion, he watched her playing what he believed to be a game of flirtation, a cruel game but not one to cause jealousy. The Ambassador was in ecstasy when he read these letters. He would shut his eyes between each sentence and kiss the paper on which they were written.

During the summer, Monsieur de   invited the Ambassador to stay with him several times in the country. They shot together in the autumn and on the days when they were not shooting Madame de   would ride with the Ambassador in the forest.

And so in the following winter Madame de   against her will had to give up hiding from herself the truth about her own feelings. She had just arrived at a place by the sea. This time Monsieur de   had not come with her. Darkness had already fallen but, she could not have said why, she wanted to go out alone. Wrapped in a heavy cloak, with some muslin round her head and her arms buried to the elbows in a fur muff, she sat by a low wall which overhung the beach and gazed on the waves and the horizon, which was lit up at regular intervals by the beam of a light-house. Suddenly she felt that she no longer had any importance ; she asked herself what she was doing in the world, and why she was living ; she felt that she was lost in infinite space; she sought for the mean-ing of life and could find no answer in her mind, only the face of one person. Her heart grew heavy with the double weight of that presence and of that absence. She felt a violent desire to be given con-fidence in her own existence and she felt that nobody could give it her but the man without whom she now knew that life would be unendurable. She hurried to the hotel, rang for her maid to pack her things and caught a train the same night.

Madame de   's return was unexpected. Monsieur de   was not at home. She wrote to the Ambassador. He came to her house at once and she threw herself into his arms. It was December, exactly a year since their first meeting and that evening at seven o'clock the Ambassador's lips, cold from wind and snow, pressed the soft lips which Madame de   abandoned to him. They loved each other so much that it seemed to them as though they could never be separated again. The warmth and the depth of their love seemed to have transported them to another world which had been created for them and into which a single kiss had opened the gate. They were oblivious of everything except themselves, their previous life was becoming unreal and Madame de   allowed a groan to escape her when she heard the clock strike half-past seven.

" Let us go to the country on Thursday," she said.

" Thursday ? " replied the Ambassador. " Three days from now ? Oh, it's so far away, much too far away "—and at that moment Monsieur de   came into the room, rubbing his hands.

Monsieur de   never lacked subjects of conversation. He talked of the theatre, the opera, of a new singer who was said to be very good, and then noticing that the Ambassador seemed not quite himself, said :

" Come down for some wild boar shooting on Thursday. It will give you a good rest."

" Thank you," said the Ambassador. " But I'm afraid I can't. I'm not free. I've already accepted another invitation for Thursday."

They talked for a few minutes about shooting and then the Ambassador left, kissing the hand of Madame de   but not daring to look into her eyes.

Madame de passed that night in a state of excitement and anxiety which robbed her both of happiness and of remorse. She stayed at home all the following day. Love made it impossible for her to apply herself to any occupation and she sat in her own small sitting-room living again the events of the day before and wondering whether they had really happened. At the end of the afternoon when the Ambassador arrived she would have liked to receive him where she was, in a room in which he had never been, but knowing that Monsieur de   would think it too intimate and would disapprove she went down to the ground floor, where the Ambassador was awaiting her in the drawing-room which led into the library.

"Come," she said, "let us go and sit in the next room."

"Why?" he asked. "Have you seen me too often in this one? I know of none that I like better. It has a quality of serious calm which makes it unlike other rooms. I see your touch everywhere and hear your laugh. Every small object here contains in

21

itself some faint reflection of your personality, so that a true artist might, I believe, by studying carefully everything that is here, be able to describe your character and draw your portrait. Tell me, why do you want to go into the library ? "

"It will be our first journey together," she answered.

He followed her and they sat side by side in two armchairs drawn up in front of a round table on which were spread some plans of battles which Monsieur de   liked studying.

Then the Ambassador said, " My love, my adorable love, for months past I have been longing to give you something I have, a jewel which is like you and which seems to have been created for you. At Christmas I shall send you one of those little souvenirs, small presents of no apparent importance, which a husband can allow his wife to accept from a friend. But this present I bring you to-day is a token of our love and that is why it is very pure, very beautiful and must remain a secret between us."

While talking he had taken from his pocket a jewel case which he now opened.

"You see these two hearts," he went on, " they are our hearts. Take care of them, hide them and above all keep them together so that you will not know one from the other. Think how happy I am to have given you something that you can wear only when we are alone."

Madame de   could hardly believe her eyes. She was unable to speak for a moment, so many thoughts flashed through her mind.

" Oh, it's not possible," she said at last, " it just isn't possible."

She threw her arms round the Ambassador's neck, kissing him and repeating " my love, my dearest love " with so much sincerity that it brought tears to her eyes. Then she got up and running to the looking glass, held up the diamonds between her first finger and her thumb close to her ears.

" No," she said, " I won't be robbed of the pride of wearing them before all the world, nor of the pleasure of hearing our two hearts whispering to me about you. Let me tell a falsehood to others, as you will always know the truth."

" A falsehood ? " he asked, smiling at the thought that there was an element of vanity underlying her desire to wear the earrings. " What falsehood do you want to tell ? "

" One that will be easily believed," she answered. " A cousin of my mother's, an old lady who likes none of her relations but me, has already given me half her jewels, and they are very fine ones. Nobody will be surprised at her having sent me these, especially now, just before Christmas. I tell you I'm her favourite. She hates my husband. They don't get on together and he never goes to see her. In fact she sees nobody. I'll call on her to-morrow in the morning,

I promise. Her life has not been happy and she will understand my difficulty."

"Happiness makes life painful by the anxiety it brings with it," said the Ambassador. "I'm so happy now that what you propose to do, frightens me. Do wait a day or two and think it over."

"No, no," she answered, "there's nothing to fear. Trust me. My cousin will love being in our confidence and I shall be glad to have someone to confide in."

"Oh, dear," said the Ambassador, "a woman cannot believe she is having a real love affair unless she has someone to whom she can talk about it."

"We are dining with you to-night," said Madame de   , "and when you see me come in, our two hearts hanging from my ears, they will tell you that we are one and that I am yours."

But he was not convinced.

"Hadn't you better go and see your cousin now at once?" he said.

"Have I time?" she said. "Yes, she lives quite close. You're right. It would be wiser. I'll go and put on my hat at once and order the carriage."

The Ambassador advised her to be careful, and left her, feeling deeply touched to have discovered, as he thought, that with all her stately beauty she was still a child at heart.

After he had left Madame de   threw the jewel case which bore the name of a South American jeweller into the blazing fire, went to her room, opened one of the cupboards of her wardrobe and hid the diamond hearts among a pile of evening gloves of a kind that she no longer wore. Presently she began to dress for dinner, did and undid her hair three times, hesitated for a long time before deciding on the dress she was going to wear, and got so late that Monsieur de ⸻, tired of walking up and down the drawing-room, came upstairs. He stood at the open door of his wife's room, tapping the floor with his foot.

"Don't get impatient," she said. "I'm quite ready. I'm just coming."

Her maid handed her a small gold chain evening bag and her gloves.

"Oh no, not those gloves," she said, "they're so gloomy," and she waved them away.

"What *does* it matter?" said Monsieur de ⸻. "We're late already. You will look very well as you are. You'll certainly look better than anyone else. That's enough. Do come along."

She took no notice but moved over to her wardrobe.

Monsieur de ⸻, annoyed, followed and caught hold of her arm to pull her away.

"Let me go, please," she said and shaking off his hand pulled out of the cupboard a handful of gloves. The earrings fell to the floor. "Oh! my hearts!" she cried, "Look, my earrings! How wonderfully lucky! It's incredible. Now I understand the whole thing. I remember that last year on the evening of the ball, I was about to choose myself a pair of gloves, just as I was this evening. You were hurrying me and in my haste I must have left the earrings among these gloves that I've given up wearing."

The lady's maid had picked up the diamonds and was looking at Monsieur and Madame de   in turn.

" Give them to me," he said to the maid, and he put them in his pocket.

" What are you doing ? " she asked.

" I'm taking care of some diamonds that you can't wear," he answered.

As they went down to the hall she insisted :

" Give me back my earrings. Why can't I wear them ? "

" If you have your secrets, I have mine," he replied.

She dared not say more. They got into the carriage and arrived at their destination without having exchanged another word.

One look which the Ambassador gave Madame de   and which Monsieur de   , without the slightest wish to spy on them, could not help noticing, confirmed the conclusion that he had come to during the drive. He remembered that the Ambassador had come a year ago from the very town in South America where the lovely Spanish lady had since been living, as he knew from the letters he had had from her asking for money. It seemed to him very probable that she should have sold a valuable piece of jewellery and not surprising that the Ambassador should have bought it. Monsieur de   was not the sort of man to indulge in romantic, platonic love affairs, but he knew that such affairs existed, and he understood how a woman must always have her little secrets, and her small regrets, sorrows and grievances, which are more easily expressed to another man than to her husband. "After a certain time," he reasoned, "husband and wife become shy of one another." The romance that had developed between the Ambassador and Madame de   was the kind of thing that even a distrustful husband could treat with indulgence. He was not surprised that his wife should have confessed to the Ambassador how she had come to part with a jewel that she loved. There was nothing in her having done so to which he could object. She was innocent and could not possibly have guessed that the Ambassador actually had in his possession the very object about which she had made her confession. "Coincidence is very extraordinary," he thought, "but perfectly natural. One can only wonder at it." He was full of common sense, and seeing the matter as he did he could find no reason to take it amiss ; he was able to distinguish between the act of a good friend and that of a guilty lover. He told himself that the Ambassador, far from having cared to offer Madame de   a present that she could not have accepted, had merely wanted to help her repair the mischief done by a falsehood of which she supposed her husband was unaware ; he could imagine how they had worked out their little stratagem, and could picture her astonishment when she saw again the earrings which she thought were lost forever. None the less, his honour forbade him to allow his wife to receive so valuable a gift from another man. So he took the Ambassador aside after dinner and led him into another room.

"My dear friend," he said, "you couldn't have acted with greater discretion, but, you see, I've good reason to know that my wife did not rediscover her lost earrings this evening among some old pairs of gloves. I wish I could believe it, but unfortunately I can't. She no doubt told you the whole story and I can well understand how you leapt at the chance which enabled her, thanks to you, to make good the sorrow she had caused me by selling the jewels I gave her as a wedding present. She thinks I don't know what she did. She told me what was untrue. She pretended that she had lost these diamonds. The reason why I have never talked to her about it is because I think there are certain matters that, if frankly discussed between husband and wife, may permanently destroy the harmony that previously existed. Nobody would be surprised to see my wife wearing these jewels because everybody knows that they belong to her; nobody would suspect that they were a present from you ! But I should of course know it and could never forget it, and you'll understand, my dear fellow, I really couldn't play the innocent to that extent. Now, I must tell you frankly that I want very much to own these earrings again, and I suggest that the simplest and the friendliest way of settling the whole matter would be for you to deposit them with my jeweller and to tell him to let me know what I owe him for them."

The Ambassador, who had listened to Monsieur

de   without interrupting him or showing
any sign of surprise or embarrassment, first thanked
him for his broad-mindedness and frankness and then
apologised for having taken part in a little plot whose
innocent intention was based on friendship. Monsieur
de   handed him the earrings and gave him the
address of the jeweller. The two men talked for a
few minutes and laughed over the childish vanity of
women, their little tricks and their illusions about the

simplicity of men. Then they joined the rest of the
company in the drawing-room, where their absence
was already being complained of, especially by the ladies,
who had felt themselves neglected. The Ambassador
sat with the group of which Madame de   was
the centre, but the evening ended without his attempt-
ing to speak to her alone.

The Ambassador felt nothing but admiration for the
way in which Monsieur de   had managed, with
great courtesy and tact, to avoid what might have
proved a disagreeable incident, but he felt at the same

time both offended and hurt by the manner in which Madame de   had treated him. Not only did he resent her words, " Let me tell a falsehood to others, as you will always know the truth," but what he found much harder, if not impossible to forgive, was that she should have accepted from him, as token of his love, something that she had previously been given by her husband, a gift that must recall to her some echo of her first love and of the earliest and happiest secrets of her married life. He felt that his own position was humiliating and ridiculous, and the love in his heart dried up at the thought that Madame de   had not minded mingling their own precious memories with others of which he could not think without suffering. Glad to rid himself as soon as possible of something which had caused him so much distress, he went to the jeweller the next morning, gave him the earrings and told him to dispose of them to Monsieur de   .

About mid-day he received a letter from Madame de   . She had not enjoyed herself the previous evening. " I hate society. I don't want to be seen by anybody but you. I feel frightened and ill when you speak to another woman," and she asked him to come to see her early that afternoon. He replied that he was very sorry to be unable to do so. " You will know how it hurts me not to see you," he wrote, " but I have had a telegram ordering me home and I must leave at once. I can only assure you that the regret with which I leave you is as intense as the love you have inspired in my heart."

Madame de   wept. The Ambassador set

forth on his journey and the jeweller called on Monsieur de   .

"Would you believe it, my dear sir," he began.

"Yes, my friend, I can believe it," interrupted Monsieur de   , in excellent humour. "I can believe it because I know all about the cause of your visit. All I have to ask you is the price of what you've brought me."

"Sir," replied the jeweller, "I wish that these jewels cost less than they do, for however much I may gain by it I feel genuinely apologetic for selling them to you for the third time. I can assure you that I was astonished to see them come back to my shop once again."

"Precious things, like people of taste, know the best houses," replied Monsieur de   .

"But what a coincidence, my dear sir. You must agree that it is a most extraordinary coincidence," said the jeweller.

"Oh," replied Monsieur de   . "I've so often had to admit that truth is incredible and that the incredible is true that I'm no longer surprised at anything."

And so he bought the earrings for the third time.

As soon as the jeweller had left him, Monsieur de   rang for a footman and asked whether Madame de   was in the house. He learnt that she had gone to her room, that she was very flushed and shivering and had gone to bed.

Monsieur de   always knocked at his wife's door, but always went in without waiting for a reply.

"Are you resting?" he asked.

"No," she replied. "There is no room in my heart either for rest or for weariness."

These words told him that she was in love, and for once he was right. She loved and was suffering from love for the first time in her life. Monsieur de   , looking down on her lying there, so beautiful, so pitiable and in such distress, tears shining in the faintly red haloes of her eyes, thought the moment had come to teach her a lesson.

He opened and laid upon the bed beside her the case containing the diamond hearts.

"What have you to say?" he asked.

She made no answer, but stretching out her hand, she took the jewels and lifted them slowly to her ears as though they were two of the kisses she remembered, the kisses that shut out the light and close the eyes.

"I'm sorry," said Monsieur de   , "but we must have a talk. Perhaps you will be good enough to listen to me for a few minutes without interrupting. You have, by your lies, made of these jewels a source of vexation. You have made me angry and you must suffer for it. As you know, my nephew's wife has just had a son. He is, alas, the only heir to our name and I've decided that we shall go to see the young mother to-morrow and that you shall make her a present of these earrings which are no longer yours."

Stifled by sorrow, shame and love, Madame de   felt that she was faced by one of those ordeals that heaven imposes on the saints. She under-

32

stood that she must submit to being brave, and that her weakness would help her. Without a word she put back the diamonds in the case and shut it. Monsieur de   laid his hand upon the lid, and said:

" That's that. You won't see them again."

The elder brother of Monsieur de   had only one son, who in defiance of family traditions and the sorrow he caused his parents, had married a very beautiful young woman, more intelligent than himself, but the daughter of a man with a bad reputation. Her father was a financier whose transactions were always of a dubious character and whose frequent speculations had resulted in a series of bankruptcies. The family suspected her of having inherited some of her father's characteristics. She had, however, behaved so well since her marriage and had proved so devoted to her home and so humble that her relations-in-law had gradually come to overlook her origin, and now that she had produced an heir to their name, nothing was too good for her.

Madame de   could not do otherwise than obey her husband and on the following day they went together to call on the young mother. They found her in bed, surrounded by relations and relations-in-law in a large, rather melancholy room, which a cradle hung with lace and huge bouquets of flowers did little to enliven. Their arrival was greeted by murmurs of affection. There was a great deal of hand-kissing and hand-shaking and embraces between the ladies. Everybody admired the baby. Madame de   bent over her niece, whispered

in her ear and slipped into her hand the present she had brought. The young mother opened the case and gave a cry of surprise and delight. The whole room was soon humming with compliments, gratitude and admiration of the diamonds, which became an heirloom from that moment. Madame de   stood apart. Her unhappy heart forced a sob into her throat and a cry of anguish from her lips. All heads were turned towards her and her niece cried out :

" Oh, my dear aunt ! "

" It's nothing, nothing," she said, " it is only the sight of this little baby—the vision of the future and the recollection of the past."

These words, coming from a woman who was generally thought to be frivolous and cold-hearted, surprised everyone. The men protested.

" The past, the past indeed. You in the full bloom of your youth and beauty. What have you to do with the past ? "

The ladies meanwhile looked at Monsieur de   ,
who slowly stepped towards his wife and handed her
a handkerchief.

" The past begins to exist when one is unhappy,"
she said to him in a low voice.

" Perhaps," he replied, " but unhappiness can be
artificial."

The coldness of his voice calmed her. She turned
to the window and looked out upon the whirling flakes
of snow like phantom dancers turning round street
corners. She stayed there with her back to the room
until her sister-in-law, laying an arm on her shoulder,
led her to the looking glass. " It's curious," said
Madame de   , " how crying always makes
one's hair untidy."

Everyone laughed and Monsieur de   said
to his brother, " She does say funnier things than
anybody."

" I hate to see her unhappy," the other replied.

Married himself to an austere lady from the
provinces, he adored his sister-in-law. She charmed
him in many ways, especially by her fashion and
elegance.

" I'm the one you ought to be sorry for," said
Monsieur de   , which provoked another laugh
and brought to a successful end a visit which had
nearly turned out a failure.

Before leaving Madame de   regretted the
absence of her nephew.

" I'm sorry not to have seen your husband," she
said to her niece, " I hoped he would be here."

" His business meetings begin at dawn," she

answered, " and go on until after dinner. I don't think he's seen his son yet by daylight."

Monsieur de   would have liked to have asked his niece some questions about her husband's business activities, but Madame de   was already standing at the door waiting for him and they left.

The Ambassador came back on Christmas Eve. He sent Madame de   a bamboo basket full of violets and mimosa. Her husband was with her, in the library, when the flowers arrived. He saw how moved she was, and left her alone.

For a fortnight Madame de   had had no news of the man who had changed her whole life, and for the moment she hardly dared touch the basket for fear there was no letter in it. Then she searched for the letter, but in vain. She wept and in her despair turned the basket upside down so that all the flowers fell to the floor. She picked up a bunch of violets and pressed them to her lips and her eyes and then, holding them to her breast in clasped

hands, she sank back on to the sofa and lay there at full length, motionless as a corpse.

Suddenly the door opened and Monsieur de came in.

" Wake up," he said, " here's a pleasant surprise for you. Take the trouble to open your eyes."

But she was lost in the cloudy regions of the heart and before she could come back to reality she felt on her hand those two lips, cold from wind and snow.

She opened her eyes and murmured, " I am taking the trouble," as she smiled at the Ambassador, whose face almost touched hers.

He looked at the flowers scattered on the carpet.

" So that's how you treat my flowers," he said.

" I've made a garden of them," she answered.

They remained, the three of them, talking for a few minutes and parted only to meet again, a few hours later, at a dinner-party in the house of some mutual friends.

Never had Madame de   appeared more beautiful than she did that evening, and there was about her an air of calm gravity that people noticed. The Ambassador did not avoid her. He talked to her of the journey he had just made and asked questions about everything that had happened in his absence. She answered him with words that meant nothing to her and hardly dared look into his handsome eyes or meet his placid scrutiny. The evening ended without his having made the slightest sign of intimacy that might have assuaged the torture she was enduring.

The Ambassador was henceforth so careful to do

nothing in public to offend her
vanity that nobody suspected
there was any change in his feelings towards her. He always
seemed glad to sit beside her, and
when they were in the same box
at the theatre or the opera, he,
standing behind her, would lean
over her shoulder to say something about the play or the
music, and it seemed to her in
the dim light that there was in
his face a gleam of that affection which he showed no more.

Madame de   suffered not only from knowing
that she was no longer loved but also from not
understanding why the Ambassador, instead of
explaining himself, avoided the woman whose heart
he had won after having courted her for so long.

For a whole year she had kept him in suspense and
when at the end of it she admitted her love, the delay
should surely have increased the value of the admis-
sion. Now, condemned to silence and feeling herself
rejected, her life seemed empty; she enjoyed nothing;
she slept badly and began to fall ill. People thought
her pallor and appearance of fatigue were due only
to the number of balls that she attended and the late
hours that she kept. It was Monsieur de   who
was the first to understand the cause of her suffering,
and he was the first to feel anxious about her.

Monsieur de   was a kind-hearted man, but
he was proud. It seemed to him quite natural that

his wife, having secretly sold her earrings, should have tried to make him believe that she had found them again; but what he found hard to forgive was that under the mask of innocence, she should have wanted to wear jewellery which another had given her, while allowing him, her husband, to remain under the illusion that it was still his gift. So, having lost his faith in her, he watched her now with mistrust. Furthermore, while his honour allowed others to enjoy the spectacle of the Ambassador dying with love at his wife's feet, he could not bear anybody to suspect for a moment that his wife was suffering from love for the Ambassador.

He therefore advised her to go away and rest somewhere by the seaside, in the sunshine she was so fond of. But she refused.

"No," she said, "the sun would tire me and the solitude would not bring me peace."

"Then do make an effort," he said, "you know how to tell falsehoods, so you ought to be capable of putting up a better pretence. And anyhow, from what is it that you're suffering?"

"From humiliation," she said.

"Because you have been found out?" he asked.

"You are quite right," she replied.

Now he himself had once suffered from this very form of humiliation and knew how hard such suffering was to cure.

"When I was a child," he said, "I once told a lie to my tutor. He was a true friend and he had trusted me. He proved to me that I had deceived him. I had to own up and the shame of it made me utterly miserable. I was deeply attached to him and I dared not look him in the face. I avoided him, I couldn't bear it, I wanted to run away and I begged my parents to send me to school."

Monsieur de   thought he had been mistaken in believing that his wife was suffering from love; he believed now that it was because she had been found out by her friend and her husband, and had in consequence been obliged to part with the jewellery, which had she been luckier she might have kept.

"I was sure that this affair would distress you," he said, "but you will soon forget all about it. You abused the good nature of the Ambassador and made him your accomplice. It was, we must face it, very naughty of you, but he has had a lot of experience of women and he's full of common sense; we've talked it over and he is not in the least angry with you,

but I can understand why you avoid him. Recover your calm, my dear, and we'll never mention the matter again."

At the end of this conversation Monsieur de   was convinced that it was not the Ambassador who was avoiding Madame de   , but she who was keeping him at a distance.

Like most people who are guided by reason, Monsieur de   was wrong as often as he was right. He wanted the Ambassador's visits to begin again and Madame de   , encouraged by some desperate hope, longed for an opportunity to explain herself, to unveil her heart to this man, whose very politeness seemed now to be based on contempt. A few days later he came to dinner and as there was some talk of an excursion on sleighs that was to take place on the Thursday of that week, she asked him whether he meant to take part in it.

" Certainly," he said, " I shan't miss it, and I trust you are going too."

" No," she replied in a low voice, " the very thought of a Thursday in the country brings tears to my eyes, now. You can understand why, I hope."

The Ambassador appeared not to have heard her, but the next evening he called. Madame de   was not expecting him. She felt very shy but made no attempt to conceal her emotion and her joy. She held out her hands, but he took them only for a moment, long enough to lift them to his lips.

" My beautiful and charming lady," he said, " I should not like there to be any misunderstanding between us."

" A misunderstanding? What a dreadful idea!" she cried. "Speak quickly so that I in turn can speak to you."

The Ambassador had his back to a white earthenware stove which set off the distinction of his tall figure.

" Come, let us sit down," she said.

" No," he replied, " I'll remain standing if you will allow me."

41

Anxious and ill at ease, she offered him a cup of tea, which he accepted, and then they stood opposite one another, silently stirring the little spoons in their cups.

"You say nothing," Madame de   said at last, "but you are here, which is all I ask. Often one is silent because one has too much to say. Don't speak. Let us only look at one another. I think that I understand."

"I will try to be brief," said the Ambassador. "When you deceived me, Madame, you struck at a feeling which you had yourself aroused in me and over which you had complete control. You drove it away—you can count on it no more. There are some memories which burn and consume, there are others which freeze and kill."

"I cannot quite understand you," said Madame de   .

"Didn't you calmly accept from me," he asked her, "a present which was closely connected with your own past life?"

"But," she exclaimed, "I had no past life any more. Nothing counted for me but you. And besides, hadn't I sold those earrings?"

"What does that matter?" he answered. "You didn't hesitate to take them from me and the first thing you did with them was to deceive me by making your husband believe that it was still he who had given them you. You made fools of us both, with as little respect for our honour as you had for my feelings."

"Penitence and forgiveness are the food of love," cried Madame de   . "Oh, pray forgive me— I lost my head. I was thoughtless."

"Thoughtless is hardly the word," he said. "No, no, you thought very quickly and very cleverly. I can still hear you saying, 'Let me tell a falsehood to others, as you will always know the truth.'" He recalled to her the whole conversation and went on sadly, "Yes, yes, nothing that you told me was true; you even invented that story of your old relation. You deceived me, you wounded me, you made me ridiculous. It takes less than that to make a man fall out of love. Your husband will never know the whole truth. He will go on believing that I was your accomplice when I was in fact your dupe. By putting yourself in a false position you put me in a grotesque one and you proved to me that you didn't love me."

"Don't believe that," pleaded Madame de   . "I was wrong, I am ashamed, I understand what you feel, but I did, I do. . . ."

The Ambassador would not allow her to finish the sentence and, as a way of preventing her from saying all she meant, he bowed, took the empty cup from her hand and replaced it with his own on the tea-tray.

There followed an unhappy and embarrassing silence. Neither knew where to look. Madame de moved to a vase and arranged some flowers. She said that hot-houses were like convents and that the flowers that came from them were better behaved, colder and more docile than those that blossomed out of doors in the course of nature. The Ambassador listened, but said nothing.

"Please don't go yet," she said. "Let us talk."

"Alas," he said, "I cannot."

At these words Madame de   abandoned all reserve and would have thrown herself into his arms, but he with great gentleness held her away.

" Are you leaving me ? " she cried. " Are you leaving me for ever ? "

" Alas," he answered, and he went.

The Ambassador was getting into his carraige when that of Monsieur de   drove up to the door. Although it was snowing heavily they exchanged civilities on the pavement.

" I've just come from the club," said Monsieur de   . " It's stifling there. I wish they wouldn't turn comfort into torture."

" Ah, the club," laughed the Ambassador. " In summer one catches cold there. It's the womb of all the draughts that afflict your delightful city."

Then, both powdered with snow, they said good-night. The Ambassador got into his carriage and Monsieur de   went into the house.

Madame de   was in her room when Monsieur de   knocked at the door and opened it.

" I've just met your suitor," he said.

" Oh, my suitor," she tried to smile, " yes, he came to see me, but I was so tired that I gave him little chance to press his suit. I'm going to bed, as you see."

Monsieur de   seemed worried about something. He had just had a heated argument at the club about an historical date and he was in a hurry to consult a reference book in the library in order to verify it. He excused himself therefore for quitting his wife so abruptly and told her the reason.

44

" Is it this date that you are worried about ? " she asked.

" No," he answered, " it's something else. But have a rest now and as we are not going out this evening we can have a quiet talk later, during dinner."

Madame de ⸻ rang for her maid and sent for writing materials. She wrote fifteen polite letters expressing her regret that she was obliged to cancel fifteen engagements. While she was writing, two

footmen arranged a dinner table by her bedside, and Monsieur de ⸻ reappeared just as one of them was bringing in the soup. Madame de ⸻ was sealing the last envelope, which she handed with all the others to one of the footmen, saying :

" Here, take this one, it's urgent, and I want it to be delivered by hand this evening," then looking at Monsieur de ⸻ she added :

"Don't be cross with me, I implore you. The slightest sign of anger, even the least annoyance, might drive me insane. Allow me to rest. Be good and try to understand me. Be kind and go out into the world for a while without me. I have not the strength to face society. I need time, I need silence, I want to forget."

"It is quite true," replied Monsieur de   , "that you have had a great deal to distress you and I think you are perfectly right not to put too great a strain on yourself. The last thing I wish to do is to bother you in any way."

"Did you find the date you were looking for?" she asked him.

"Yes," he said, "it was, in fact, only verifying a certainty, but now that I've done so, and have nothing on my mind, I can talk to you more freely about a family matter. My brother is worried about his son. The boy, as you know, is as honest as he's stupid, but he's entirely under his wife's influence. She's charming, I agree, but her father is barely respectable and my brother is afraid that between them they may have got the boy involved in some shady transactions. He doesn't know anything definite. It's only suspicion, but he's naturally worried to death about it. He wanted to avoid irritating his son by seeming to interfere in his private affairs, so he has asked me to have a talk with him, and try to find out how things are. I meant to do it to-day, but I couldn't get into touch with him. I've been looking for him everywhere. I've called twice at his house and this evening before going to the club I had a long talk with his wife, but

I couldn't get the conversation round to what I wanted to know. She wouldn't let me ask any questions about her husband's affairs, and I left her knowing no more than when I arrived. I had also the disagreeable impression that he was in the next room all the time and had been listening to what we were saying. She has only been up for two days and I must say she was looking very beautiful, more so than she used to, as though the birth of her child had altered and improved her. Perhaps she was only putting on an act for my benefit, but she seemed to be so happy and at peace with the world, thinking of nothing but her home and her baby. She's coming to see you as soon as she can go out ; she seems very anxious to do so."

Monsieur de   added a few banal remarks about the danger of marrying out of one's class and expatiated on the value of ancestors as guarantees.

" If I didn't know who my parents and grandparents were," he said, " I feel that I shouldn't know who I was myself."

Madame de   had not interrupted, merely signifying by gestures and smiles that she was listening. She shut her eyes occasionally and as soon as dinner was over Monsieur de   , anxious not to tire her, wished her good-night and ordered his coffee to be served in the library, where he had letters to write.

Madame de   had always been very fond of her old nurse, who had remained in her service as housekeeper. She would often send for her in the evening while she was dressing for dinner, and they would talk about fashions and recipes, and of the people they had known in the past, and memories of

47

old days. She sent for her that evening and although it was not her habit to take people into her confidence she said :

" Nannie, I'm so unhappy that I'm no longer even bored. I feel that I'm wearing a heavy mantle of sorrow which protects me from everything. Can you understand that ? I feel that nothing can do me harm any more, but that something might do me good. Can you understand ? Life becomes very interesting when one feels one is dying. What do you think ? "

" I think you've always had ideas that don't make any sense," the nurse answered. " Your real trouble is not having children, and you ought to be saying your prayers instead of muddling your head."

" But I'm not muddling my head, Nannie. I'm very unhappy."

" You're unhappy because you muddle your head," the nurse answered, and then she told her of several pilgrimages which cured barren women. She made her drink a tisane, turned over and smoothed her pillows, opened the window, shook the curtains to change the air more quickly and put the flowers outside.

"Go to sleep," she said, "and you'll be better to-morrow."

For three weeks Madame de   had only left her bed to lie on the sofa and had only left the sofa to go back to bed when, at the end of February, her niece came to see her. She felt at once that there was something on her niece's mind that she wanted to talk about, but for a long time they merely said polite things to one another without coming to the point. At last Madame de   , feeling that her niece could find no way of opening the subject that was on her mind, thought she might help her by complaining that her nephew never came to see her. The niece blushed, sighed deeply and, recovering herself after a moment's silence, said :

"Don't be cross with him, Aunt, I beg of you. He loves you very much and, as for me, although I know you so little, I've come to you as being the only member of the family who doesn't frighten me and who might be able to help us. You give me courage and I feel that your great beauty must make you able to understand everything."

"What is it that troubles you ? " asked Madame de   .

Then the niece told her sad story.

"We are on the verge of disaster," she said. "My

husband, who is inexperienced and has no gift for business, has become involved in a series of speculations which he thought were sure to make our fortune, but which have in fact completely ruined us. To-day we are on the eve of a scandal and he dares not tell his parents. My father has given me a large sum, but it's not enough, and I've come to ask you, dear Aunt, whether you would, very secretly, buy those earrings you gave me. It would save us."

"My poor child," replied Madame de   , "what you tell me is too terrible. I would give everything that I have in the world to be able to help you, but, alas, I have no private fortune except what belongs to your uncle, over which I have no control. But do let me tell him about your troubles. He's a generous man and less severe than you suppose."

"No, no, Aunt, please, please do anything rather than that. He would think it his duty to tell my father-in-law. My husband would be disgraced and they would say it was my fault, that he should never have married me, and there would be a family drama which would be more than he could bear. No, we must try to get out of it without hurting anybody."

Madame de   longed with all her soul to own those two diamond hearts so intimately bound up with the memory of the only man she had ever loved.

"If I bought them," she said pensively. "I could never wear them, and they would regain all the deep meaning that they have for nobody but me."

Her niece listened to her in astonishment, having no idea what she meant.

"But what are we to do, Aunt?" she asked.

Madame de   advised her to go and see the family jeweller.

" He's a man on whom you can completely rely. He's a trustworthy friend and I believe he will be able to do for you what I am so very sorry that I cannot do myself. But tell me, dear child, won't your parents-in-law be very surprised never to see you wearing the earrings? "

"Oh, they won't have the chance of being surprised," she answered. " We've decided to settle down in the country permanently. My husband will devote himself to looking after his estates, which will delight his parents. When we are in the country, I shall say that my diamonds are in the safe in town, and when we are in town I shall pretend to have left them in the country. That can go on for years."

Madame de   had been deeply moved as she listened to her niece.

" Don't misunderstand me," she said, " I am truly sorry for you. I'm always sorry for people who make mistakes. I wish I could feel sure that my affection would be of some use to you. And now you must hurry off and lose no time. Let me know as soon as you can if everything is all right."

She rang and ordered her carriage, telling her niece to take it and keep it as long as she needed it.

When the niece opened the case that held the diamonds in front of the jeweller, there was little explanation needed.

"I want to sell them," she said. " I'm sorry to have to do so. They were given to me when my son was born. I know that I can count on your discretion."

The jeweller, whose business it was to know everything, was aware that Monsieur de   's nephew was threatened with bankruptcy and he was also aware that a fashionable marriage was about to take place in the wealthiest society of the town. He was sure that such a magnificent present would make a strong appeal to a rich young man at the moment when he most wanted to dazzle his future bride. The earrings therefore came to the jeweller at the right moment and he had no hesitation in buying them. Madame de   's carriage brought back a note from her niece. " Thank you," she wrote, " our troubles are at an end."

The jeweller, however, sat looking down at the earrings which lay on the table between his elbows while he rested his head on his hands. Few people knew that Monsieur de   had given his niece the earrings which had so often shone in the ears of Madame de   , and the jeweller was thinking that if he now sold them without Monsieur de   's knowledge he might be accused of having done harm to the credit of his good customer. Reluctant to betray the confidence of a young lady who had turned to him in a desperate situation, he searched for some way in which he could, without violating his conscience, contrive to let Monsieur de   know that the earrings were once more in the market. Finding no solution of the problem, he thought that he might have either to keep them himself or get one of his colleagues to put them up for sale in another continent. He thought the matter over for several days and as the result of his reflections decided to consult Monsieur de

Monsieur de   had one cause for satisfaction and another for annoyance. He was irritated by the way in which Madame de   was behaving. She had imprudently received a certain number of visitors and so the rumour had got about that her withdrawal from society was not due to ill-health but to melancholy, and as the Ambassador appeared sometimes at the club and sometimes in the drawing-rooms of other ladies at the hour at which, as everyone knew, he had been wont to call on her throughout the past year, Monsieur de   was afraid that his wife's retirement would be attributed to the Ambassador's infidelity. He therefore urged her to go out more and was annoyed by her persistent refusal to do so. He believed that she was blaming herself for what had after all been only a truly feminine and touching error, committed in order to avoid hurting her husband. Not forgetting how sensibly he had himself behaved in forgiving the man who had involved himself in a conspiracy that might have led to a duel, he resented the Ambassador's altered behaviour, which, hardly noticeable at first, was now all too evident, and he considered it an incivility both to his wife and to himself. He could well understand, without admitting it, why Madame de   refused to parade her defeat before the jealous eyes of those who had envied her. All this somewhat took away from the pleasure with which he had recently received a good piece of family news. His elder brother had come to tell him of his son's decision to give up business altogether and live in the country. Monsieur de   's elder brother, delighted by this unexpected decision, had sat for two hours by Madame de   's sofa while she feigned surprise and asked him for every detail.

" Oh, the sly little creature," she said, " she gave me no clue as to what she was scheming."

Monsieur and Madame de   learnt that their nephew and niece had left that morning, taking the baby and all their belongings.

" I gave them everything they asked for," said

Monsieur de   's brother, " and I did it the more gladly because of the anxiety I had suffered. I admit that remorse for having lacked confidence in my own son made me all the more generous."

" I can perfectly understand your feelings," Madame de   answered.

" And now they won't hear of living in town," Monsieur de   's brother went on, " my daughter-in-law whispered to me as she left, 'Our happiness will be safer in the country.'"

" She is a very intelligent girl," said Monsieur de   . " We are not to blame for having mis-trusted her at first. One cannot feel confident about somebody one doesn't know, but now I do know her, I think her both wise and reliable, and I'm sure that she has an excellent influence on your son. Without her he would never have taken this sensible decision."

So it was that when the jeweller called he found Monsieur de   a happy brother but an exasperated husband. Nevertheless, he was well received and in-vited to sit down by the library fire.

" Well," my good friend," said Monsieur de   with a smile, " what can I do for you to-day ? "

" I have come to ask your advice," replied the jeweller. " I am in a most delicate position ; in order to avoid doing something that might give you great offence, I have to betray another's confidence and my conscience is most uneasy."

Monsieur de   was amused.

" You alarm me," he said, " Tell all, I long to hear."

" Well, here's the problem that has been keeping me awake at night," the jeweller began. " Your niece, my dear sir, has sold me those famous earrings. Everybody in the business world was aware that your nephew was on the verge of bankruptcy, so I avoided asking the young lady any questions that might embarrass her. I was sure that she was selling the jewels to save her husband, and she has, in fact, saved him. And now I have the chance of re-selling these admirable diamond hearts to one of your young cousins, whose engagement will probably be officially announced this evening."

"So I believe," interrupted Monsieur de   , "his father is my first cousin and we are very fond of the young man."

"I feared that you might be offended," the jeweller went on, "if I were to get rid of the diamonds without warning you. I didn't even know that you had given them to the young lady and I was frightened at the thought of creating a false impression in the minds of people who, seeing that they were in my possession, might think that you had been forced, for certain reasons, to part with them."

"Your reasoning was very sound," Monsieur de   answered. "I am most grateful. Thanks to you, I shall be able to give great pleasure to my wife, whose melancholy and ill-health are not altogether unconnected with the regret she has felt at being without her beloved earrings for over a year."

Monsieur de   bought the diamond hearts and the jeweller apologised for selling them to him for the fourth time. They shook hands like men who feel that fate has thrown them together and that they are sure soon to meet again.

After the jeweller had left, Monsieur de   sat down again by the fire and, leaning back in his armchair, remained for a long time with his eyes shut while his fingers beat a tattoo on the jewel case that lay on his knees.

Before going to his club he looked in on his wife and stood for a moment in front of her with one hand hidden behind his back.

" If I do you a great favour," he asked, " will you do me one in return ? "

" Certainly," she answered, " if there is any favour which can still give me pleasure."

He gradually revealed the hand he was hiding, and calmly laid the diamond hearts in the trembling hands which Madame de   held out to him.

" Are they mine ? How can they be mine ? " she cried, without even thinking to thank him.

Monsieur de   made her promise to keep the secret and told her what he had just learnt.

" My nephew behaved like a lunatic and his wife too. They deceived my brother and I'm going off now to tell him the truth. It's my duty, in the first place, to warn him in case his son should do something equally mad again, and in the second place you can't wear the earrings so long as he believes they belong to his daughter-in-law."

" I see the situation quite differently," she replied. " These children were very foolish, but now they have at last acted sensibly. You know your brother and how he is guided by his principles rather than by reason. Why renew his suspicions of his son, who now deserves his confidence ? What is done cannot be undone. Let us say no more about it. They must have suffered a great deal already. Why plunge them back into the misery from which they have just escaped ? "

" You are perfectly right," said Monsieur de   . " You are really kind, and true kindness of heart is a better guide than reason or principle. But what am I to say to my brother about the earrings ? "

" You can tell him you have had replicas made of them," said Madame de   , but then catching herself up immediately, she cried, pressing both hands to her heart. " No, no—let us have no more lies. Time will pass and everybody will forget. Who is going to see me anyway ? I don't go out any more, as you well know."

" I will say they are replicas, yes," said Monsieur de   , " because you are going out, you are indeed ; that is the favour that I am asking you to do me in return for the one I have just done you."

"I'm not going out any more," said Madame de   .

"Then give me back the earrings," Monsieur de   ordered.

"No, never," she answered, "Let me keep this memory of the past."

"If you feel so strongly, think of the future. Protect yourself and protect me. Show some gratitude and promise me that you will come with me to-morrow evening."

"Very well," she said, "I promise."

"Be sensible," he continued, "and use your reason. Look at the position you have put me in and the position in which you have put a good friend who wanted only to do you a service. If you appear at last wearing these earrings you will set his conscience at rest, and mine too, and you will dissipate a disagreeable atmosphere from which we have all been suffering and for which you alone are responsible."

Madame de   knew the real truth. She knew why the Ambassador had left her, but she could neither explain this to her husband nor could she bear to part with the diamond hearts. They were the token of her only great love. They brought back to her ears the passionate words and to her lips the burning kisses. When Monsieur de finished speaking she made a slight sign with her head, which had to suffice him. He had no wish to argue with her. For him, all that mattered now was that the Ambassador should see Madame de wearing the jewels which nobody but her husband had the right to give her.

The health of Madame de   had been seriously
affected by all that she had suffered and by a month's
confinement to her room. Monsieur de   ,
paying little heed to this and none to the bitterly
cold February weather, insisted on her going to the
ball. It was given by those cousins of Monsieur
de   to celebrate the engagement of their son.
Here it was that Madame de
appeared in the magni-
ficent sunset of her beauty.
Because she felt so near to
collapse, she held herself
with more than her accus-
tomed pride and dignity.
Smiling she arrived, the diamonds sparkling in her ears,
and she was still smiling
when her eyes met those of
the Ambassador. The smile,
the diamonds, with the deep
weariness that she was concealing, lent her an air of

haughtiness, almost of defiance, or so it seemed to the
Ambassador, who believed that by wearing the
diamonds she wished to prove that the past was
obliterated and he no longer counted for anything
in her life. Later, when he bent over her hand which
she held out to him so tenderly, he said :

" I will never forgive you," and, while others
crowded round her, he withdrew.

Monsieur de   , his pride satisfied, was in the
best of good humours. He was ready to sit up till

morning, and although he was usually most courteous he forgot for once about his wife and allowed her to go home without him.

As Madame de   lay sobbing in her bed, she abandoned, almost unconsciously, all hope and all desire. She understood that having first forfeited the Ambassador's faith she had now lost his respect, because by continuing to wear the earrings she had seemed to profane all that remained of their love.

" Come and see me," she wrote to him. " Come, oh, come. You have misunderstood everything. Come, I pray of you. If you have ever loved me, grant my prayer."

She thought that despair was the cause of the high fever that held her, so that the least movement of her hand made her shudder, and every shudder sent a stabbing pain through her heart.

She waited long for the return of Monsieur de   and then, having given him time to go to bed, she threw a cloak over her shoulders, and taking the letter in her hand, regardless of the bitter wintery weather, she left the house by the first light of the February dawn.

The hall porter who rose to open the front door for her was the sole being who saw her go.

" Madame," he cried, " oh, Madame, wait, wait."

" I must go," she said, " I am coming back."

As she sped across the town in the unusual light of early morning the snow began to fall. She stopped at last before a gloomy, grand front door. She rang the bell and when there was no reply she went on ringing furiously and began to cry out, " Open the door—open it."

Frozen and shivering she continued to ring and to call out until at last a sleepy servant, half-dressed, in a

stately uniform appeared. He took the letter from her hand and slammed the door in her face.

When she came home that morning Madame de   was dying. There was nothing left that could tempt her to live. The cruel winter had been more than she could bear and now she was bound elsewhere. When three days later the Ambassador replied to the entreaty she had sent to him by coming in person, she was hardly alive.

"My wife can see nobody," said Monsieur
de   .

"She has sent for me," said the Ambassador. He
held her letter in his hand.

The desperate condition of Madame de   did
not admit of argument. Monsieur de   had to
respect her last wishes, and he led the Ambassador
to the bedside of the woman who had so longed to
see him again, but would never do so.

Madame de   was already putting on the
marble beauty of death.

The two men stood motionless, facing one another
across the bed, looking down on her. She was still
breathing feebly in faint, irregular gasps. Presently,
feeling that this was no place for him, the Ambassador
was about to withdraw when Madame de   ,
with a convulsive gesture of death agony, stretched
her long arms straight out on either side of her body
and with one last deep sigh was dead. At the same
moment her two clenched hands gently opened and
disclosed a diamond heart in each. It was as though
she had meant to give them away to she cared not
whom.

The raised eyes of Monsieur de   and the
Ambassador met.

"She is dead," said Monsieur de   . "Take
this heart which she has given you. The other is
her own. I will take charge of it."

The Ambassador took the heart which Madame de
         held out to him. He kissed the hand of the
dead woman and left the room. He went straight to
the jeweller's.

63

" Fasten this diamond heart on to a thin gold chain and fasten the chain round my neck so that it can never be undone. Do it quickly, for I have no time to lose."

When that had been done he went straight home, gave certain instructions and, while his luggage was being packed, sent off a number of telegrams. Then he left the country.

But Monsieur de   laid the other heart on the heart of his wife and then sent for the old nurse. Forthwith the room was full of the rustle of skirts and the sound of wailing. The candles which had so often lit up her dinner parties now shone round her deathbed. Monsieur de   sent for his tailor and, without telling him the reason, ordered some suits of mourning.

Vilmorin.   Madame de.

Redwood Library and Athenaeum
NEWPORT, R. I.

—

Selections from the Rules

New fiction is issued for 7 days, new non-fiction for 14 days, and other books for 28 days with the privilege of renewal.

Books overdue are subject to a fine of 2 cents a day.

All injuries to books and all losses shall be made good to the satisfaction of the Librarian.

5 volumes may be taken at a time and only 5 on 1 share a subscription.